IF I RAN

The ZOO

By Dr. Seuss

RANDOM HOUSE · NEW YORK

For TONI *and*

MICHAEL GORDON TACKABERRY THOMPSON

This title was originally cataloged by the Library of Congress as follows:
Geisel, Theodor Seuss. If I ran the zoo, by Dr. Seuss [pseud.] New York, Random House [1950] I. Title.
PZ8.3.G276If   50-10185   ISBN: 0-394-80081-8 (trade); 0-394-90081-2 (lib. bdg.); 0-394-84545-5 (pbk.)

Manufactured in the United States of America

"It's a pretty good zoo,"
Said young Gerald McGrew,
"And the fellow who runs it
Seems proud of it, too."

"But if *I* ran the zoo,"
Said young Gerald McGrew,
"I'd make a few changes.
That's just what I'd do . . ."

The lions and tigers and that kind of stuff
They have up here now are not *quite* good enough.
You see things like these in just any old zoo.
They're awfully old-fashioned. I want something *new!*

So I'd open each cage. I'd unlock every pen,
Let the animals go, and start over again.
And, somehow or other, I think I could find
Some beasts of a much more un-usual kind.

A *four*-footed lion's not much of a beast.
The one in my zoo will have *ten* feet, at least!
Five legs on the left and five more on the right.
Then people will stare and they'll say, "What a sight!
This Zoo Keeper, New Keeper Gerald's quite keen.
That's the gol-darndest lion I ever have seen!"

My New Zoo, McGrew Zoo, will make people talk.
My New Zoo, McGrew Zoo, will make people gawk
At the strangest odd creatures that ever did walk.
I'll get, for my zoo, a new sort-of-a-hen
Who roosts in another hen's topknot, and *then*
Another one roosts in the topknot of his,
And another in *his,* and another in HIS,
And so forth and upward and onward, gee whizz!

But that's just a start. I'll do better than *that*.
They'll see me next day, in my zoo-keeper's hat,
Coming into my zoo with an Elephant-Cat!

They'll be so surprised they'll all swallow their gum.
They'll ask, when they see my strange animals come,
"Where *do* you suppose he gets things like that from?
His animals all have such very odd faces.
I'll bet he must hunt them in rather odd places!"

And that's what I'll do,
Said young Gerald McGrew.
If you want to catch beasts you don't see every day,
You have to go places quite out-of-the-way.
You have to go places no others can get to.
You have to get cold and you have to get wet, too.
Up past the North Pole, where the frozen winds squeal,
I'll go and I'll hunt in my Skeegle-mobile
And bring back a family of *What-do-you-know!*
And that's how my New Zoo, McGrew Zoo, will grow.

I'll hunt in the mountains of Zomba-ma-Tant —
With helpers who all wear their eyes at a slant,
And capture a fine fluffy bird called the Bustard
Who only eats custard with sauce made of mustard.
And, also, a very fine beast called the Flustard
Who only eats mustard with sauce made of custard.

I'll catch 'em in caves and I'll catch 'em in brooks,
I'll catch 'em in crannies, I'll catch 'em in nooks
That you don't read about in geography books.

I'll catch 'em in countries that no one can spell
Like the country of Motta-fa-Potta-fa-Pell.
In a country like that, if a hunter is clever,
He'll hunt up some beasts that you never saw ever!

I'll load up five boats with a family of Joats
Whose feet are like cows', but wear squirrel-skin coats
And sit down like dogs, but have voices like goats —
Excepting they can't sing the very high notes.

And then I'll go down to the Wilds of Nantucket
And capture a family of Lunks in a bucket.
Then people will say, "Now I like that boy heaps.
His New Zoo, McGrew Zoo, is growing by leaps.
He captures them wild and he captures them meek,
He captures them slim and he captures them sleek.
What *do* you suppose he will capture next week?"

I'll capture one tiny. I'll capture one cute.
I'll capture a deer that no hunter would shoot.
A deer that's so nice he could sleep in your bed
If it weren't for those horns that he has on his head.

And speaking of horns that are just a bit queer,
I'll bring back a very odd family of deer:
A father, a mother, two sisters, a brother
Whose horns are connected, from one to the other,
Whose horns are so mixed they can't tell them apart,
Can't tell where they end and can't tell where they start!
Each deer's mighty puzzled. He's never yet found
If *his* horns are *hers,* or the other way 'round.

I'll capture them fat and I'll capture them scrawny.
I'll capture a scraggle-foot Mulligatawny,
A high-stepping animal fast as the wind
From the blistering sands of the Desert of Zind.
This beast is the beast that the brave chieftains ride
When they want to go fast to find some place to hide.
A Mulligatawny is fine for my zoo
And so is a chieftain. I'll bring one back, too.

In the Far Western part
Of south-east North Dakota
Lives a very fine animal
Called the Iota.
But I'll capture one
Who is even much finer
In the north-eastern west part
Of South Carolina.

When people see *him*, they will say, "Now, by thunder!
This New Zoo, McGrew Zoo, is really a wonder!"

Most beasts are quite friendly, but still, in some lands
Some beasts are too dangerous to catch with bare hands.
For those that are ugly and vicious and mean
I'll build a Bad-Animal-Catching-Machine.
It's rather expensive to build such a kit,
But with it a hunter can never get bit.

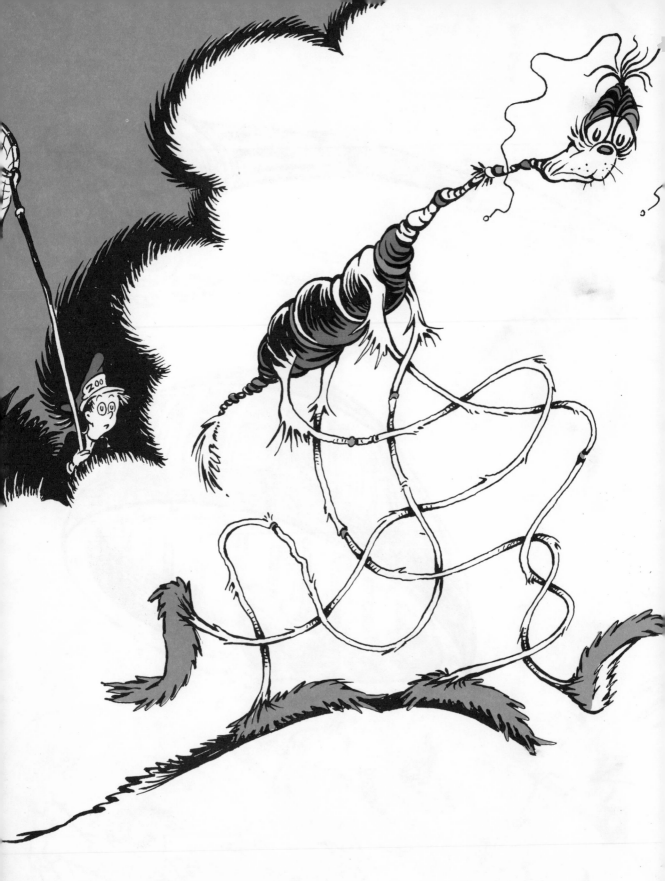

A zoo should have bugs, so I'll capture a Thwerll
Whose legs are snarled up in a terrible snerl.

And then I'll go out and I'll capture some Chuggs,
Some keen-shooter, mean-shooter, bean-shooter bugs.

I'll go to the African island of Yerka
And bring back a tizzle-topped Tufted Mazurka,
A kind of canary with quite a tall throat.
His neck is so long, if he swallows an oat
For breakfast the first day of April, they say
It has to go down such a very long way
That it gets to his stomach the fifteenth of May.

I'll bag a big bug
Who is very surprising,
A feller who has
A propeller for rising
And zooming around
Making cross-country hops,
From Texas to Boston
With only two stops.
Now *that* sort of thing
For a bug is just tops!

And when I've caught *him,*
Then the next thing you know
I'll go and I'll capture
A wild Tick-Tack-Toe,
With X's that win
And with Zeros that lose.
He'll look mighty good
In this Zoo of McGrew's.

I'll bring back a Gusset, a Gherkin, a Gasket
And also a Gootch from the wilds of Nantasket.

And eight Persian Princes will carry the basket,
But what *their* names are, I don't know. So don't ask it.

In a cave in Kartoom lives a beast called the Natch —
That no other hunter's been able to catch.
He's hidden for years in his cave with a pout
And no one's been able to make him come out.
But *I'll* coax him out with a wonderful meal
That's cooked by my cooks in my Cooker-mobile.

They'll fix up a dish that is just to his taste;
Three chicken croquettes made of library paste,
Then sprinkled with peanut shucks, pickled and spiced,
Then baked at 600 degrees and then iced.
It's mighty hard cooking to cook up such feasts
But that's how the New Zoo, McGrew Zoo, gets beasts.

I'll go to the far-away Mountains of Tobsk
Near the River of Nobsk, and I'll bring back an Obsk,
A sort of a kind of a Thing-a-ma-Bobsk
Who only eats rhubarb and corn-on-the-cobsk.
Then people will flock to my zoo in a mobsk.
"McGrew," they will say, "does a wonderful jobsk!
He hunts with such vim and he hunts with such vigor,
His New Zoo, McGrew Zoo, gets bigger and bigger!"

And, speaking of birds, there's the Russian Palooski,
Whose headski is redski and belly is blueski.
I'll get one of *them* for my Zooski McGrewski.

Then the whole town will gasp, "Why, this boy never sleeps!
No keeper before ever kept what *he* keeps!
There's no telling WHAT that young fellow will do!"
And then, just to show them, I'll sail to Ka-Troo

And

Bring

Back

an IT-KUTCH

a PREEP

and a PROO

a NERKLE

a NERD

and a SEERSUCKER, too!

I'll hunt in the Jungles of Hippo-no-Hungus
And bring back a flock of wild Bippo-no-Bungus!
The Bippo-no-Bungus from Hippo-no-Hungus
Are better than those down in Dippo-no-Dungus
And smarter than those out in Nippo-no-Nungus.
And that's why I'll catch 'em in Hippo-no-Hungus
Instead of those others in Nungus and Dungus.
And people will say when they see these Bips bounding,
"This Zoo Keeper, New Keeper's simply astounding!
He travels so far that you'd think he would drop!
When *do* you suppose this young fellow will stop?"

Stop . . . ?

Well, I should.

But I won't stop until

I've captured the Fizza-ma-Wizza-ma-Dill,

The world's biggest bird from the Island of Gwark

Who only eats pine trees and spits out the bark.

And boy! When I get *him* back home to my park,

The whole *world* will say, "Young McGrew's made his mark.

He's built a zoo better than Noah's whole Ark!

These wonderful, marvelous beasts that he chooses

Have made him the greatest of all the McGrewses!"

"WOW!" They'll all cheer,
"*What this zoo must be worth!*
It's the gol-darndest zoo
On the face of the earth!"

"Yes . . .
That's what I'd do,"
Said young Gerald McGrew.
"I'd make a few changes
If *I* ran the zoo."

BOOKS BY DR. SEUSS

And to Think That I Saw It on Mulberry Street
The 500 Hats of Bartholomew Cubbins
The King's Stilts
Horton Hatches the Egg
McElligot's Pool
Thidwick The Big-Hearted Moose
Bartholomew and the Oobleck
If I Ran the Zoo
Scrambled Eggs Super
Horton Hears a Who
On Beyond Zebra
If I Ran the Circus
How the Grinch Stole Christmas
Yertle the Turtle and Other Stories
Happy Birthday to You
The Sneetches and Other Stories
Dr. Seuss's Sleep Book
I Had Trouble in Getting to Solla Sollew
The Cat in the Hat Songbook
I Can Lick 30 Tigers Today and Other Stories
The Lorax
Did I Ever Tell You How Lucky You Are?
Hunches in Bunches
The Butter Battle Book

BEGINNER BOOKS

The Cat in the Hat
The Cat in the Hat Comes Back
One Fish Two Fish Red Fish Blue Fish
Green Eggs and Ham
Hop on Pop
Dr. Seuss's ABC
Fox in Socks
The Foot Book
My Book About Me
Mr. Brown Can Moo! Can You?
Marvin K. Mooney, Will You Please Go Now?
The Shape of Me and Other Stuff
There's A Wocket in My Pocket
Great Day for Up
Oh, The Thinks You Can Think
The Cat's Quizzer
I Can Read With My Eyes Shut
Oh Say Can You Say?

3